Library of Congress Control Number: 2020923527

ISBN: 978-1-68369-266-9

Printed in China

Typeset in Miller and Gill Sans

Designed by Ryan Hayes
Story adapted by Rebecca Gyllenhaal,
based on the film written by Mike White
Production management by John J. McGurk

Quirk Books
215 Church Street
Philadelphia, PA 19106
quirkbooks.com

10 9 8 7 6 5 4 3 2 1

School of Rock

Based on the film written by Mike White

Illustrated by Kim Smith

QUIRK BOOKS
PHILADELPHIA

Dewey had only two dreams in life: to be a rock star
and to win the Battle of the Bands.

Instead, with just three weeks until the big competition,
he was kicked out of his own band.

Even his best friend thought it was time for Dewey to quit music.

"Maybe it's time to give up those dreams," Ned said.

Dewey didn't want to give up on his dreams. But maybe everyone was right. Maybe he didn't have what it took to be a rock star.

So, instead, he became a substitute teacher.

"You'll be teaching a fifth grade class," said Principal Mullins. "You'll have to be strict and firm with the children."

Principal Mullins introduced Dewey to the class.
"Students, meet Mr. S. He's going to be your
teacher until the end of the quarter. You have
a lot of material to cover, so I'll leave you to it."

Dewey didn't care about the curriculum or Principal Mullins's rules.

"As long as I'm here, there will be no grades and no detention," he said. "We're gonna have recess all the time!"

All the kids cheered. They'd never had a teacher like Mr. S before!

The next period was music class.
Dewey listened through the door.
It gave him an idea . . .

"I heard you in music," Dewey said. "You can really play!
So we're starting a new class project. It's called . . . ROCK BAND!
We only have three weeks until the Battle of the Bands, so let's get to work!"

Dewey showed Zack how
to hold an electric guitar.

He put Lawrence
on the keyboard.

Katie traded her cello for a bass guitar.

And Freddy used his cymbals skills to master the drums.

Soon everybody was rocking out!

"What are the rest of us supposed to do?" asked Frankie.

"Rock bands need so much more than just musicians," Dewey said.
"There's a job for everyone!"

Marta, Alicia, and Tomika volunteered to be the backup singers.

The roadie crew was in charge of the band's equipment: amps, lasers, and smoke machines.

Billy got to work designing the band members' costumes.

And the security team made sure that Principal Mullins didn't find out they were skipping their other lessons.

But Dewey soon learned they had a big problem. None of the kids had ever listened to rock music before!

So he got to work teaching
the class rock 'n' roll history.

The band was sounding better and better every day.
But something was still missing.

"Rock is about the passion, people!"
Dewey said. "Where's the joy?"

But we're playing
it perfectly!

That's the problem! Rock ain't about doing things
perfect! It's about sticking it to the man! If you
wanna rock, you gotta break the rules!

"What's 'sticking it to the man'?" asked Summer.

Dewey said, "Sticking it to the man is when you tell the grown-ups how you really feel! But instead of crying or pouting, you say it with a song!"

"Now what makes you mad more than anything in the world?" Dewey asked.

You!

No allowance!

"All you have to do is turn your feelings into a song."

"All right!" said Dewey.
"That was a perfectly decent rock song!"

The next day, Summer showed Dewey the name they had come up with for the band.

"It's perfect!" Dewey said. "And we shall teach rock and roll to the world . . . "

♪ ♪ *There's no way you can stop the School of Rock!* ♪

Zack also had something to tell Dewey.
He had written a song for the band!

Rock got no reason
Rock got no rhyme!

"That totally rocks!" Dewey said.
"Everyone, we're learning Zack's song!"

But Dewey had forgotten about something very important: Parents' Night. It was the same evening as the Battle of the Bands.

When the parents found out what Dewey had been teaching their kids, everyone started yelling at the same time.

Dewey grabbed his guitars and took off.

But the kids made a decision. They had worked too long and too hard to miss playing in the show. They snuck out of school while their parents were busy yelling at Principal Mullins.

The bus driver was waiting in the parking lot. Summer told him to pick up Dewey on their way to the Battle of the Bands.

"Listen, I'm sorry I used you guys," Dewey said. "And I'm sorry I lied."

"There's no time for apologies!" said Summer. "We're going to be late!"

They made it to the show just in time. But backstage, Tomika pulled Dewey aside. She said that she couldn't go onstage and sing.

Dewey told the band that they were going to play Zack's song.

"But we haven't practiced that one as much," said Zack. "If we play my song, we might not win!"

"We didn't come here to win," said Dewey. "We came here to play one great show. And one great rock show can change the world! So, let's get out there and melt some faces!"

When the School of Rock took their places, a murmur went through the crowd. Some people even laughed. They weren't expecting a bunch of kids to compete.

But soon after the music began, everyone was cheering. The School of Rock was blowing everybody's minds!

The parents and Principal Mullins
pushed their way through the crowd.
They wanted to put a stop to the show.

But when they heard the music the children were making, all they could do was listen. They couldn't believe how talented their kids were. Or how much fun they were having!

Tomika sang the chorus.

Zack played an amazing guitar solo.

And Dewey body-surfed
through the crowd!

The School of Rock didn't win the Battle of the Bands.
But the crowd chanted their name until they played an encore!

Now Dewey teaches an after-school music class called the School of Rock. And he has a new dream: sharing his love of music with other people.